JN022917

雨 の 合 間

Lull in the Rain

津 川 エ リ コ

Eriko Tsugawa

ミツイパブリッシング

トニーと太郎へ

For Tony and Taro

目次

Contents

雨 の 合 間

Lull in the Rain

カタツムリ

カタツムリ
苦しんでいる

闇を好むその身を
夏の朝の陽にさらして
緑の泡を口から吹いている

夕べ撒いた青色の駆除剤を
食べたに違いない
今は無言で苦しんでいる

緑いろの泡が止むと
二、三のハエが現れた
死んでいくものを調べるために

玉虫色のコルセット
ブンブンうなって死の舞踏
一つの死は彼らの複眼の中に増殖する

カタツムリ
午後には乾いて縮み

重みのない自分自身の殻の中で
ほとんど消し去られ
ごみ粒のように見える

Snail

Snail
in agony

exposing her cryptozoic body
in the heat of the early morning sun.
Green foam blowing from the mouth.

She was tempted
by a blue pellet, sprinkled last night,
and is writhing in pain.

When the green bubbles
stop seething, a few flies emerge
to investigate a dying thing.

Each, buzzes and dances a 'danse macabre',
dressed in an iridescent bodice. One death,
reflected as many, in those compound eyes.

By the afternoon the snail,
dried out and shrunken,

almost obliterated
in its own weightless shell,
looks like any speck of dirt.

ページをめくる人

最後の行に来るたびに
母の手がタイミングよくページをめくる

私は読むのを止めその染みのある手を眺める
青い静脈が薄い皮膚から盛り上がり

枝分かれしてやがて消えていく
関節は固く蛇の抜け殻みたいに曲がって

見慣れた風景
これらは私の手だ

それなのに死んだ母の手と見分けがつかない
母は私の為にページをめくろうと帰って来るのだ

Page Turner

Each time I reach the last line
my mother's hand turns the page like a score turner.

I stop reading and watch an old freckled hand.
The blue veins raised through the thinned skin,

Branching out until they fade away.
The knuckles, stiff and bent like a snake slough.

Familiar terrain.
These are my hands but so often

I can't tell these from my dead mother's.
She comes back to turn the page for me.

雨の合間

誰とも同じように
ナメクジとカタツムリもお使いに行こうと

雨の合間を待っていて濡れそぼった
繁みから這い出てきた

舗道に出てすぐ誰かに踏みつぶされたり
自転車に轢かれたりした

良く晴れた翌日
ナメクジはコンクリートの上で

黒いダリアの押し花みたいだった
微かなスジの細部をあらわして

Lull in the Rain

Just like any of us who waited for
a lull in the rain to go on our errands,

the slugs and snails too, have now come out
from the soaked bushes.

Some are crushed right away underfoot
or run over by bicycles on the pavement.

After one fine day, I noticed
a dark dried slug stuck to the concrete that

looked like the pressed petal of a black dahlia
with some faint details of striped vein.

アタカマ砂漠で骨を探す女たち
ドキュメンタリー「ひかりのノスタルジア」に因んで

　アタカマ砂漠で人間の骨を探す女たちはみなエキスパートになる。どんなに小さな骨でも彼女らは見落とさない。それらは彼女らの父であったり、祖父であったり、夫であったり、息子であったり、兄であったり、弟であったり、妹であったり、友達であったりするのだから。彼らは不穏分子として捕えられ拷問され「死のヘリコプター」に乗せられて、太平洋やアンデスやアタカマ砂漠に捨てられた。これを命じた独裁者にとって批判は犯罪だったのだ。

　アタカマ砂漠のパラナル天文台では天文学者が空の彼方に新しい星や命の存在の可能性を探している。大型の望遠鏡が人間の目では見られないものを探している。

　砂漠の花、パタ・デ・グアナコはアタカマで十日間だけ花を咲かせる。エルニーニョ現象が僅かな湿気を美しい予感のように運んできて、それを感知したパタ・デ・グアナコがうす紫の花を咲かせる。水分はここではすぐに蒸発してしまう。死体も十日のうちには枯れた木のように乾くだろう。

　女たちが素手で砂を掘り、死のかけらを探しているときに、パラナル天文台の科学者は宇宙の何処かに別の命が存在するはずだと言っている。砂漠は骨を探す女たちにとって天文学者にとっての宇宙と同じぐらいに無限なのだ。

注＊独裁者とはチリの軍人ピノチェト（1915-2006）。
彼は1973年、クーデターで社会主義政権を倒し、
1990年まで軍事独裁政治を行い非人道的にジャーナリストや左派を弾圧した。

Women Who Look for Bones in the Atacama Desert

(After documentary: 'Nostalgia for the light')

Those women who look for human bones in the Atacama Desert, all become experts. They don't miss the tiniest pieces of bone, as these are the bones of their fathers, grandfathers, husbands, sons, brothers, friends and sisters, all captured, tortured, killed and thrown from a death-helicopter into the Pacific, or the Andes or the Atacama. For the dictator who ordered this, criticism was a crime.

In the Paranal observatory in the Atacama Desert, astronomers are looking for new stars and the possibilities of life beyond the sky. The very large telescope can see things that human eyes can't.

The desert flower, Pata de Guanaco found there, blooms pale purple for ten days. It detects the beautiful prospect of the slightest moisture during El Nino. Ten days here, withers human bodies too.

Scientists in the Paranal observatory hope to find new life in the universe, while women are digging the sand with their bare hands to find some fragment of death.

For those women who look for human bones, the Atacama is as infinite as the universe is for astronomers.

Note: Dictator – Augusto Pinochet(1915-2006). In 1973, commanded a coup to overthrew Allende's socialist government,forming a Military Dictatorship. He inhumanely oppressed the left and journalists.

コスモス

八枚の花びらのうちの三枚が
失敗した折り紙みたいに折り曲げられて
隣の二枚は破れている
昨日はきれいに揃って開いていたのだから不思議だ
たたまれた花びらの内側を好奇心から覗いてみた

見てごらん
淡い淡い緑の毛虫が一匹
ひかりに晒されて身をよじらせ
ガクと花の間に
あわてて身を隠した

毛虫は昼寝を覚まされたかな
食べ物の花びらは寝床の傍にあって
もし毛虫さえその気なら
寝床だって食べられる

Cosmos

Three out of eight petals of a cosmos,
were folded in, like poor origami
and two beside were tattered.
I wondered why, as it was open fully yesterday.
Curiosity made me look beneath the folds.

Lo!
A tiny caterpillar of palest green, now exposed,
wriggled out of the light.
Then hurried to hide herself
between the calyx and the flower.

She was caught napping.
She has her food beside her bed
or she can eat her bed, too
if she so pleases.

壺

その壺が二つに割れた時
闇は抜け出した
二つのかけらは静かに取り残された
蝮の脱け殻のように

石に刻まれた砂漠の王の
開いたままの目
二つの破片は開き続ける
一つの貝のように元に継ぎ合わされることは二度とない

壺は
熟した梨の実のように落ちて割れた
収穫は甘く
朽ちは素早く

庭の隅の灰の中に半ば埋もれ
雨が降って空洞の目があふれると
性懲りもなく泣き続けた

Vase

When the vase broke in two,
darkness sneaked out.
Two pieces lay there silent
like the cast-off skin of a viper.

There was a king who was carved in stone
with eyes permanently open in the desert.
Like his eyes, two halves stay open
never to be joined again like a sea shell.

The vase,
having fallen like a ripe pear and split,
harvest-sweet,
decays fast.

Thrown in the ash-pit, now half buried
when it rains the empty eyes overflow
and continue crying tirelessly.

儀式

あなたが毎日泣くというのは
ほんとうだろうか

夫が仕事に出かけ
自閉症の息子が迎えのバスに引き取られ
一人になると

あなたはカーテンを閉め息子のベッドで
ひとしきり泣くのだと言った
気が済むとあなたの一日がはじまるのだと

今日私はあなたを訪れた
ドアを二度叩き
返答がなく私は去った

ドアをもう一度叩くことがどうしても出来なかった
あなたが泣いているかも知れないと思ったのだ
「今日は本当に暑かったですねえ」そう言おうと思っていただけ

涼しい夕暮れの風が
汗ばんだ私の首を掠めていった
「今日は本当に暑かったですねえ」

Ritual

Is it true that you cry
every day?

Your husband gone to work,
your autistic son picked up by the school bus
and you now alone in the house.

You close the curtain, lie on your son's bed to
cry for a while and when consoled, your day truly starts.
So said you to me.

Today, when I visited,
I knocked on the door twice
then left with no response.

I couldn't knock once more as I thought
you may be crying. I was just thinking of saying
'It's very hot today, isn't it?'

Cool evening breeze now
brushes my sweaty neck.
'It was very hot today, wasn't it?'

浜辺

私の足の裏が浜辺で
何かガラスの破片のようなもので本当に切れた

本当にというのはそれが起こるのではと
想像していたからだ

引いていく波の泡の中に
血が混じった

手にしたサンダルを白旗のように上げて
私の先を歩いていく二人の友を私は呼んだ

何かを察した一人は
怪訝な顔つきで近づいてきた

私は突然鋭くなった足の痛みを意識しながら
もう一人の立ち止ったままの人の夕日に晒された横顔を見た

流れ出る血の帯が臍の尾のように
海に落ちる夕陽と繋がっていった

Beach

On the beach, I stood on a piece of broken glass
and it cut my sole, indeed.

Indeed? Yes, I had imagined
that might happen, and it did.

My blood mixed with the ebbing water
in the froth.

I called my friends, two men walking ahead of me
and waved my white sandals in surrender.

One of them sensed something wrong and
walked towards me with a puzzled look.

I watched the other man's profile reflected
in the evening sun and felt a sudden sharp pain in my foot.

The ribbon of my blood in the sea water connected
with the sinking sun's reflection like an umbilical cord.

菩提樹の木の根元に

地上に晒された菩提樹の太い根と根の間に
きちんと台形の形をした小さな石
半分は埋まって古い墓石みたいだった

ミニチュア墓石は二センチ半ぐらいで
アリかミミズの名のない墓といったところだ
誰かがここで泣いただろうか

地上に盛り上がった菩提樹の老木の根と根の間を
アリは匂いを追って上ったり下ったり忙しい
私が墓と思ったその石に
無関心で動揺することもなく

At the Root of a Lime Tree

A tiny stone, perfectly trapezoid in shape
between the exposed roots of a linden tree,
half buried, looked like an old grave stone.

A miniature grave without an inscription,
an inch high, for an ant or an earthworm.
Did anyone weep here?

Ants are busy climbing up and down scent trails
between the exposed roots of the old linden tree,
seemingly indifferent, untroubled by the stone that
I thought a grave.

遠くの村

私たちは最終駅で降りたのでした
座礁した船を見るためです
絶え間ない波の鞭が船の錆びた背骨を打ち
あなたの手が私の手を握りました

永遠に繰り返される懲罰でもあるかのように
その鞭が振り下ろされる度にあなたの怯むのが
絡ませた指から伝わりました

そうでした
私たちは再び列車に乗ったのでしたね
二人とも窓側に席をとって

あなたは列車が遠ざかっていく方を
私は列車が進んで行く方を見
列車が曲がるときには先頭の金属の車両が私の体の延長のように
伸びていくようでした

列車はあまりに海近く走ったのでしぶきが窓ガラスを打ち
私たちはそれを避けようと無駄に身をよじり固く笑いました
ガラスの泡は獣の濃い涎のように流れ

列車は遠い村にむかってゴトゴト鈍い音で進みました
傾くときには二度と元に戻らないように思いそれでも必ず
元に戻りその度に私には何かがこぼれたように思えたのでした

私たちは何も話す必要のない姉と弟のように静かでした
遠い時代の二人の囚人のように足首を鎖でつながれて

Distant Village

We got off the train at the terminal to see
the old shipwreck run aground.
We watched the tireless waves lashing
the rusty metal bones and you held my hand.

At each whip-cry of the waves
I felt you flinch through our entwined fingers
fearful of this perpetual punishment.

That's right,
we took the train again, didn't we?
We both sat by the window.

You, looked back at what the train was leaving behind,
I, looked towards the train's head, visible on the curve,
the metal carriages, an extension of my body,
stretching, stretching away...

The train ran so close to the sea that the spray hit the window.
We dodged to avoid it and our smiles were stiff.
The froth on the window streamed down like bestial saliva.

The train thudded on towards our distant village.
Tilting, it seemed it might never return, yet
it did, but I felt that each time something was spilt.

We were silent like a sister and a brother with no need to talk,
like two prisoners of olden times, fettered at the ankles.

虫殺し

虫を殺した
とがった鉛筆の芯の先で

小さな虫だった
人がまだわたしをきれいだと言っていた頃

なんと彼らは間違っていたことだろう
わたしは醜かった

別のときには
紙の上から潰したこともあった

もったいぶった占い師の顔つきで
体液の小さな滲みの形をしらべたのだった

人差し指でも殺した
あまりに小さいのでそれは簡単だった

それでも平気だった
人がまだわたしをきれいだと言っていた頃

なんと彼らは間違っていたことだろう
私は醜くそれを知っていた

虫はどこかへ急いでいたが
私がそこへは辿り着かせなかったのだ

ぷつんぷつん遠くの花火のような
命の途切れる音がして

そのときは自分の肺の気胞も
1つ潰れている筈だった

Insect Killer

I killed an insect
with a pencil's tip.

I killed a tiny one,
when people still said I was pretty.

How wrong they were.
I was ugly.

Another time I crushed one
under some paper

and I examined the fluid stain
with the face of a solemn fortune teller.

I killed one with my forefinger, too.
It was easy and

I was indifferent,
while people still said I was pretty.

How wrong they were.
I was ugly and knew that.

The insect looked as if in a hurry to go somewhere,
but it never got there.

There must have been a snapping sound
of death, a distant firework.

One of the air sacs in my lung
also collapsed each time.

アウシュヴィッツの死体運搬人
ハンガリー映画「サウルの息子」に因んで

父たちを見た
母たちをみた
妹たちを、弟たちを、祖父母たちを
友人たちを、近所の人たちを、そして彼らに交じる知らない人たちを
彼らの目は見開かれていて陽のない空が映っていた
彼らの目は二度と閉じないだろう

私たちはソンダーコマンドー、死体運搬人
一人は足首をつかみ、私は腕を持ち、
揺らして一、二、三で壕の中へ
死体、死体、また死体
深く広い溝は裸の死体で満たされ
作物のように山積みになった
壕を囲む兵士は自分の収穫に無関心だった

私は酒宴の音楽を毎晩聞いた
陽気な笑い声に続く笑い声を聞いた
ライ麦パンがざっくり切り取られ赤ワインがグラスから溢れた
踊っているものもいるに違いない
重い靴が床板を鳴らした
その時、機関銃が彼らの「乾杯！」と同時に打たれるのを聞いた

逃亡者だ
逃亡者だ
照明が逃亡者の刺青の番号を照らした
綿密な記録のために

Sonderkommando

after the Hungarian film 'Son of Saul'

I saw my fathers.
I saw my mothers.
I saw my sisters, brothers, grandparents,
my friends and neighbours, tangled amongst strangers.
Their eyes were all open, the sunless sky reflected in them.
These eyes would never be closed.

We, Sonderkommandos, I grabbed the ankles and another
held the arms of a naked body and we swung,
one, two then three, into the pits.
Bodies, after bodies, after bodies.
The deep and wide ditches soon filled and
naked bodies were piled like crops.
The clothed stood around, indifferent to their abundant harvest.

I heard festive music every night.
I heard merry laughter.
The sourdough rye cut casually and red wine poured to the brim.
Some were dancing as the wooden floor drummed with heavy boots.
Then I heard the machine-gun shots
Synchronized with their cries of 'Prost'.

There was a runner.
There were runners.
Their tattooed numbers on their arms were checked
against the exact records.

私は冬の焚き木のように重ねられた
無数の死体の中に妻を見つけた
白い枝々は絡まっていた
彼女の剥き出しの腕は私を彼女の横に招くかのように上がっていた
「知っているよ、お前は結婚指輪を編んだ髪の中に隠したね。
でも、彼らはお前の頭を剃ったのだった」

それから私は息子の死体を見つけた
彼の肌は初めて触れたときのように柔らかかった
お前が生まれた日、お前の母が痛いほどに美しい笑顔で
「息子に自己紹介なさい」と私に命じたのだよ
息子よ、私はお前の傍に立っている一つの死体だ

注＊ソンダーコマンド：強制されて死体運搬に従事した強制収容所の収容者。

I saw my wife among the bodies
piled like fire logs for winter.
Untrimmed white branches entwined.
Her bare arms up as if inviting me to lie down beside her.
'You hid our wedding ring in a plait of your hair,
but they shaved your head.'

Then I found my son's body.

His skin still as soft as the day I first touched it.
That day your mother with a painfully beautiful smile,
commanded me 'Introduce yourself to your son'.
My son, I am a dead body standing beside you.

Note: Sonderkommando: Concentration camp inmates,
forced to work for the Nazis on the disposal of bodies.

貝殻

降りていくと海と砂ばかりだった
何百もの白い小さな貝殻が散らばっていた

同じ形の2枚の貝が開いたまま未だ繋がっていて
まるで渡りの蝶が濡れた砂浜でひと時休んでいるようにも

あるいは荒野で稀に咲くという葉も茎も無い花が
たった今開いたというようにも見えた

幾度も波にやさしく撫でられて陽の下に晒され
どの貝も窪んだ方を下にして横たわっていた

これらを踏まずに歩くことは不可能で
最も薄いガラスが踏まれ割れていく音を聞くのだ

これらはやがて砂の一部となる
内臓は小さくてほんの少ししかないが

波に流されチドリに食われて
貝は空っぽで清潔な事この上ない

Seashell

It was all sea and sand when I went down and
hundreds of tiny white seashells everywhere.

Two identical wings still attached and opened wide, as of
migratory butterflies taking a brief rest in the wet sand.

Or those rare desert flowers, without leaves or stems,
that have just appeared after many years.

Exposed by the gentle strokes of a wavelet
all lie hollow side down.

It is impossible to walk the beach without crushing them
and I hear the sound as of the thinnest glass squashed.

These will soon be a part of the sand.
As all the internal organs though so small

had been eaten by plovers or washed away,
shells are empty and clean and cleanest.

キャラメル

朝早く
舗道に
キャラメルが落ちている
ひとつ、ふたつ、みっつ…
ひとつずつ紙に包まれたまま

昨日ここを子どもが走った！

Toffee Drop

Early in the morning
on the pavement,
I found some toffees.
One, two and three....
each one individually wrapped.

Yesterday, a child ran along here!

こんなにも濃い青

　同じ通りに住むジョンが亡くなったとき、青いトルコ桔梗の花束を彼の奥さんのローナに持って行った。彼女はそれを気に入ってくれたようで、何週間か経って道端で会ったとき、「花がとてもきれいだったわ。ユーストーマはとても長く持ったの」と言った。

　私はそのときはただ頷いて、家に帰ってからユーストーマと言う名を調べた。それがトルコ桔梗の正式な名前だった。

　ローナは運転しないのだけれど、ジョンの車はまだ家の前にある。そこを通るときジョンが運転手席にいてハンドルを握りながら何か新しいいたずらを考えているのではないかと思う。彼は天気のいい日にはしょっちゅう彼の家の門の前に出ていた。
「ジョンさん、元気？」
「ああ、僕はまだ地面の上だ」そう言って微笑むのが常だった。前歯に欠けている歯があってそれが彼を腕白な少年みたいに見せるのだった。

　今日、花屋の前でトルコ桔梗をまた見つけた。立ち止まって暫く眺めていた。ローナのユーストーマ、私のトルコ桔梗は本当に濃い青だった。

Blue So Intense

When John, on our road passed away, I brought a bunch of blue Turkish bellflowers to his wife Rhona. She liked them. When I met her a few weeks later, she mentioned them again. 'Those Eustoma lasted a long time. They were very beautiful'.

I just nodded, but I checked the name 'Eustoma' at home and it turned out that's the proper name for Turkish bellflower.

John's car is still at their front gate though Rhona doesn't drive and when I pass there, I feel he is in the driving seat and thinking of doing some new mischiefs. He was often outside the gate of his house when the weather was good.

'Hi John, how are you?'

'I am still above ground' he used to say, smiling. His missing front tooth made him look like a naughty boy.

Today I saw some blue Turkish bellflowers in a shop again and stopped to look. Rhona's Eustoma, my Turkish bell flowers, blue so intense.

点字

病院のベッドで退屈から
彼女は萎びた乳首をもてあそんだ

彼女の目には眼帯がしてあって出来ることがあまりなかった
ラジオは聞きたくなかった

彼女は逃げやすい乳首の点を押す
二つの言葉を打つ点字なのだ

1つは「本当に」もう一つは「さようなら」
言葉は熟したアケビの濃いミルクのように滲み出し

あばら骨のそれぞれの盛り上がりをなぞって
果汁はゆっくり流れる

注 * アケビ：蔓科の植物でチョコレート蔓として知られる。
果実は甘い果肉を含み季節の珍味として日本で食用される。

Braille

In her hospital bed, out of boredom
she fingers her withered nipples.

With her eye patched, she can't do much else.
She doesn't want to listen to the radio.

She pushes the evasive nipple-dots,
feeling out two words in braille

One 'good', the other 'bye'.
The words emerge like Akebia's thick milk.

This succulence flows slowly,
tracing the swell of each rib.

Note: Akebia Quinata, a climbing plant commonly known as Chocolate Vine.
The fruit contains a sweet soft pulp, eaten in Japan as a seasonal delicacy.

凍った湖

凍った湖に私は戻ってきた
走っては滑り走っては滑る
氷の上ひどくぎこちなく

ほんの数メートル
でもこれで十分なのだ
子供みたいな気分にさせてくれる

風が私の白い髪を通り抜け
耳の端を凍らせる
私は凍った湖に戻ってきた

厚い氷の下の水は見えず音もない
子供のとき、氷の中に囚われた泡を人の目玉だと思ったっけ
昔、この湖のそばで虐殺があったと母さんが言った

男は沈んで女は浮かび子供は川の方へ流れたんだ
湖を囲むトウヒの木は人間なんだよ
みんな家族を失った者だから湖のそばを離れないんだ

冬になって凍った木が割れるときには
人の叫びのような甲高い音でこだました
それは私たちを眠らせなかった
私にはその古い話を伝える娘がいない

自分の息が白いヴェールのように空中に浮かんでいる
それを裂いて私は進む
走っては滑り走っては滑る氷の上

Frozen Lake

I have come back to the frozen lake.
I run and slide, run and slide,
so clumsily on the ice.

Only a few meters I slide,
but far enough
to exhilarate me like a child.

The cool wind goes through my white hair
and freezes the edge of my ears.
I have come back to the frozen lake.

Invisible water under the thick ice, mute.
I used to see the trapped bubbles as human eyes
as Mother spoke of carnage at the lake shore.

'Men sunk, women floated and children carried away to the river.
All the dark spruces surrounding the lake are the bereaved
and they never leave the shore.'

I remember those trees cried out in winter with a human voice
when the sap inside froze and split them.
Their shrill echoes didn't let us sleep and
I have no daughter to tell that old story to.

Now, my breath, white, floats in the air like a veil.
I move through to rend it
and run and slide, run and slide on the ice.

眠い

若いホームレスの二つの膝の間に
うとうとしている頭が落ちる

コンクリートの舗道
小さな段ボール紙に腰をおろし

膝を立てコンビニストアの壁に寄りかかったまま
汚れた右手で紙コップをどうにか持っている

青年はどうしても眠気に勝てない
立てた膝と膝の間にこっくり彼の頭が落ちる

紙コップの底には二つか三つの銅貨があるっきり
誰かがもう一つコインを投げ入れた

チャリンという音
あまりに微かで彼を起こさない

Sleepy

Between his knees
a young homeless man's nodding head falls.

On the concrete pavement
he sits on some cardboard

leaning against the shop wall near the doors,
his soiled right hand holds a paper cup.

He can't resist his sleepiness at all,
head falling between his knees.

A few coppers at the bottom of the cup
and someone adds another.

A chink so faint,
it doesn't wake him.

殺し方

ビールが効くという人がいるのはそれがナメクジには抵抗し難いからだ
銀色のねばねばした跡は彼らの長引いた苦しみを語っている
ある人は自分では殺せないカタツムリを線路のある崖下へ抛り投げている
戻ってこないことを望んで

別の人は深夜に懐中電灯で狩りをする
カタツムリは夜型で捕まえ易いのだ
彼女はプラスチックの袋に入れてそれらを「収穫」という
彼らは窒息死するだろう

カタツムリの前菜はギボウシで主菜はヒエンソウ
そのあとのデザートはタチアオイだ
時々、私はカタツムリをスコップで切ったり石で潰したりする
そして土を被せる

庭は何百という軟体動物の死の上に成り立っている
春の新芽は埋葬場から出てくる
土砂降りのあとのある午後、私は一匹のナメクジを見つけた
白いサンザシの花びらを食べていた

このあまりに質素な食べ物を私はうっとり眺めた
ナメクジは何も殺さず落ちているものを拾うだけだ
この白い小さなナメクジが白い花びらの具現でないならば
他の一体何だろう

ナメクジよ草地へお行きと私は言った
そこで人間に邪魔されることのない宴を開くのだよと

How to Kill

They say 'beer is best'. Irresistible to slugs,
but slimy silver trails tell of their prolonged agony.
A friend throws her snails down a steep railway slope,
hoping they don't come back.

Another collects them at midnight with a torch,
when they are most active and easy prey.
She says 'harvest' and puts them in a plastic bag,
where they suffocate to death.

A snail's starter, a Hosta undulate, for main course,
a blue delphinium, digestive hollyhock comes later.
Sometimes I crush a snail with a stone or chop a slug with a spade
and cover them with soil.

So, the garden stands over hundreds of mollusc deaths,
A burial ground where new spring shoots emerge.
Then one afternoon after heavy rain, I found a slug on the path
eating the white petal of a hawthorn.

I watched in raptures at her simplest of meals.
She didn't kill anyone and was just gleaning.
If this tiny white slug is not the embodiment of the white petal,
then what would it be?

So, I urged her, 'Go to a meadow and have a banquet,
where there is no human harassment'.

カモメ

二羽のカモメが煙突の上で啼いている
海はそんなに遠くはないが近くもない
彼らがどうしてここまで来るのか私は知らない

煙突の上からそうは多くは見えない
何本かの街路樹と遠くの丘
それに疲れているみたいな歩行者だけ

カモメよ
ここにはお前の食べるものなんか無いよ
ニシンの目玉がほしいんだろうに

二羽のカモメが屋根の上で啼いている
彼らの声を聞いたコマドリとシジュウカラが
深い繁みに隠れる

Seagulls

Two seagulls on the chimney mew.
The sea, not far away but not so close either.
Why they come here I don't know.

They don't see much from the chimney,
only some trees, the hills in the distance
and sparse, tired looking pedestrians.

Seagulls,
here offers nothing you could eat.
You want herring eyes, don't you?

Two seagulls on the roof-top mew.
Robins and tits who hear their cry
hide in the thick bush.

ウズ川

夕べの激しい雨で
川の水は土手まで
上がってきている

川は泥に色をつけられて
速い流れに
混ざっている毟られた草は青い

胸にきつく手を当てて
心臓の音が一つ一つ水の上にこぼれて
いくのを私は防いでいる

流れの中に半分隠れて
半分見えている白い顔

彼女はウズ川に入った
土手の草の中に予め隠しておいたいくつかの石を
──それは彼女が人生で感じた持ちこたえた最後の重さだったのか──
コートのポケットに詰めて

高潮が彼女を上流へ運んで
遊んでいる子供たちが河原に俯せの彼女を見つけた
ワラの案山子だと思ったらしい
石はポケットに残っていた

彼女は海へ行かなかった
それが八十年前
今日も土手を浚って流れは速く
毟られた草は青い

The River Ouse

After last night's torrential rain
the river runs as high as the rim
of the embankment.

The mud-coloured water
flows fast and torn grasses
mingled there are green.

I place my hands on my chest
to prevent my heartbeats, from spilling
one by one into the water.

I see the white face half-hidden,
half-visible in the stream.

She went into the river Ouse,
putting some stones in her overcoat pockets,
from where she had hidden them in the grass,
the last weight she held in life.

The high tide pushed her upstream.
Some kids found her
and thought her a stray scarecrow.
The stones still remained in her pockets.

She didn't go to the sea.
Eighty years ago, that was.
The running river eats at the bank even today and
the torn grasses green.

十月の風

今夜はどこで眠るのかなどとは訊かないで
濡れた路地で眠らずにいるか雨漏りのする屋根の上で

鼻の欠けたガーゴイルと彼の見た七百年の
悲惨な歴史について話していよう

それとも人なき谷間で緑の長い草を鞭打って
一晩で白く染めてしまおうか

今夜もまた眠られずにいる者の目を覚まさせ続け
嘆きの歌で動揺させ何度も寝がえりを打たせよう

冷たい星を闇の中でさらに光らせ
落ちてくる光を夜明けまでに貪り食らおう

私の母は誰なのかとは訊かないで
彼女はただもう冬の匂いに過ぎないのだから

かつてないこの夜をむしろ眠らずにいたい
闇を抱えて冷たい石を飛び越えながら

岸辺に沿って次から次へ
鉄色の水にさざ波たてて

October Wind

Ask me not where I sleep tonight.
I rather stay awake in a wet alley or on a leaky roof talking to

a deformed, nose-chipped gargoyle, about the calamities
he has seen over the last seven hundred years.

Or rather dye the long grass white overnight
whipping at tufts in uninhabited valleys.

I'd wake all who are sleepless again tonight
and toss them, disturbing them further by the song of my wails,

and let the cold stars glitter more in the empty
as I devour fallen rays till the dawn.

Ask me not who my mother is as she is no more.
She is no more than a scent of winter.

I rather stay awake on this unexampled night
saving the dark and leaping over cold stones,

along the shore, one after another
rippling the iron dark water.

母さんが昨日死んだ

母さんが死んだ
五年前の十月の昨日
朝早く

母さんは姉さんの家に運ばれて横たえられた
その晩、私は母さんの家に行って
一人で缶ビールを飲んだ

もっとビールか何かはないかと冷蔵庫を開けた
食べ物がいっぱい詰まっていた
一週間は買い物に行かなくても生きられる筈だった

漬物をつまんで
賞味期限の切れたヨーグルトを
ひとさじ、ひとさじ、またひとさじ

母さんが死んだ
五年前の十月の昨日
私は自分を母さんのベッドに横たえた
四年ぶりの帰省だった

Mother Died Yesterday

Mother died yesterday
this month of October, five years ago.
It was early in the morning.

She was brought to my sister's house and laid out there.
That night I went back to mother's house alone with
a can of beer and drank it to numb my feelings.

I opened the fridge looking for more beer
or anything and it was full with food.
She could have lived another week without shopping.

I ate some pickles,
some out-of-date yogurt
a spoonful, another spoonful and another spoonful.

Mother died yesterday
this month of October, five years ago.
That night I laid myself out on her old bed.
My first-time home in four years.

寒い四月

きっと昨日の寒さだろう
クマンバチが死んでいた
二匹は路上でもう一匹は裏庭で
私は拾ってコットンの上にのせた

そのうちの一匹は前肢がコットンに引っかかって
逆立ちしていた
毛だらけのお尻が宙に突き出している
花の芯に突っ込んでいるときみたいに

ほんの昨日のことだった
クマンバチが台所に飛び込んできて
きっと道に迷ったのだろうと外に追い出した
寒さを予測して避難してきたのだと今になって思う

寒い四月はクマンバチを殺す
私の収集は三匹で始まったが
きっとどこかにもっとあるだろう
これに含まれるのが

Cold April

It must be last night's cold that
killed the bumble bees I found.
Two on the road, one in the back garden.
Now collected and laid in a cotton bed.

One of them stands on his head
with front legs snagged in the cotton.
His hairy bum up in the air
as if he is diving into a flower heart.

Only yesterday I noticed a bumble bee
come into the kitchen and I ushered it out
thinking it must have lost its way.
Now I realise that bee just foresaw the need for shelter.

Cold April kills bumble bees, and thereby
started my collection with three.
There must be more hereabouts,
for inclusion.

お椀の雪

　早くに亡くなったお父さんのことを話してくれた人がいる。彼女がまだ小さい女の子だった頃、東京に稀な雪が降って、お父さんが彼女に見せるために庭からお椀に雪を盛って持ってきてくれたということである。きっと白いご飯のように見えたことだろう。実際、彼女はその思い出の中の白い雪をご飯のように食べて生き続けて来たのではないだろうか。

　時として私は若くして死んだ父と自分自身を彼女の思い出の場所に置き換えてみることがある。父は私に話しかけることが無かった。私が幼過ぎたのだ。

　母は父の死後、父のすべての写真を燃やしてしまった。それには彼女自身の正当な理由があった。だから思い出す父の顔がない。父は失われてしまっているのだ。だが私もお椀の雪がほしいのだ。今でもいつまでも父にねだり続けている。お椀は空である。

A Bowl of Snow

Somebody once told me about her father who passed away prematurely, when she was a young girl. One day it snowed in Tokyo and her father brought a bowl of snow from the garden to show her, as snow was a rare occurrence there. It must have looked like a bowl of rice. This is intriguing as rice is our staple food and it appears to me that she has been sustained by that memory of a bowl of snow.

Sometimes I imagine myself in her place with my own father, who himself died very young, before I was old enough to converse with him.

My Mother burnt all photos of him after he died. She had her own reasons. So, I don't have an image to recall his face. He is lost to me. I too, would like to have a bowl of snow. I'm forever asking him. The bowl, still empty.

雲を追って

　老いた俳優が舞台の上で、桟敷席辺りに浮かんでいるらしい架空の雲の行方を追っている。彼の視線が上目遣いに右から左へと移動し、それと同時に頭が回転する。

　観客は雲の存在を俳優の視線の中に見ていて、彼はスポットライトの中央で黒い斑点のように立っている。その彼が舞台の縁に近づいて、前列と二列目、おそらくは三列目の座席の観客たちが彼の骨ばった頬骨に涙が流れるのを見るかも知れない。彼の目の中の雲は行ってしまったようだ。

　彼は無残に折れた木のようにしばらく身を固くして立っている。それからつばのある帽子を脱ぐために腕が動く。彼の白髪の頭がガクンと落ちるのはまるで操り人形のようである。これが彼のお辞儀。終わりを示すお辞儀なのだ。

Chasing the Clouds

An old actor on stage traces the movement of imaginary clouds floating around the balcony. He casts his eyes upward, from right to left, as his head turns.

For the audience, the clouds appear in his eyes and he stands like a dark patch in the centre of a spot light. Now moving closer to the edge of the stage, the people in the front row and the second row and maybe the third, see the tears rolling down on his bony cheeks. The clouds seem to be gone now from his eyes.

He stands stiff for a few seconds like a mauled tree, then his arm moves to take off the flat cap. His white head drops abruptly like a marionette. This is his bow. His bow to signal the end.

マグパイ

私の足音を聞いてマグパイが草むらから飛び上がった
そんなに遠くへ行かずに低い塀の上に止まったのは
また地面に戻るつもりなんだろう

マグパイよ、
お前の好きなものは何だ、虫か、ベリーか
お前の縄張りでどんな鳥がどこで巣を作っているか全部知っているね
親鳥が雛に与えるエサを探しに行っている間、
雛も何匹かはお前の手にかかることだろう

Magpie

Magpie sprang up from the grass as I approached.
It didn't move far and stopped on a low fence,
planning its return.

Hey Magpie!
What is your favourite food, insects or berries?
You know the nest of every bird around here and
when parents leave the nest to gather food for their young,
I know, you will take some of those chicks too.

蛍

シャーラが河川敷の方へ私たちを案内した。蛍が出ていることを期待して。でも去年見た時期から二週間も早いということだった。

いた、いた、気の早い蛍はいた、暗い藪の中に。突然ついた明かりが遠くの流れ星みたいに数秒飛んだ。ここにもあそこにも。そんなに多くはなく、中には藪を離れてしばらくふらふら飛び空中へ消えてしまうものもいた。

一匹捕まえた。

「アッチイ、アッチイ」

私が叫びみんなが笑った。

「生物発光だから熱くはないはずだ」

そうだ、ただの化学作用で冷たい光なのだ。でも私には本当に熱く感じられた。愚かな心理作用だ。

暗い海に点滅する灯台が今、私の手の中にある。私は自分のこぶしを緩めるためにもう一方の手でこぶしの檻を覆った。すると緑色の夜光が指の間から洩れた。

灯台のように蛍にも個々の発光のパターンがあるという。そのパターンを知る前に、私はその蛍を放してやった。そしてひとしきりよろよろと飛ぶその蛍のあとを追った。手のひらの窪みに蛍が残していった想像上の熱をまだ感じながら。

Fireflies

To the river base, Shara brought us, hoping the fireflies would be there. She said that this was two weeks earlier than she had seen them last year.

All of a sudden, there they were, in the dark bushes. One hasty firefly lit up and flew for a few seconds, like a shooting star, afar. More here and there too, but not so many, as some flew off leaving the bushes and disappearing into space.

'Ouch, hot!',

I caught one and panicked as it felt hot. The others laughed. 'Bioluminescence isn't hot!'

Yes, it is just a chemical reaction, the light is cool no matter how hot I felt it. Just my silly psychology.

A light house in a dark sea held inside my fist. I covered this cage with my other hand to loosen the fist, then the luminous green leaked through the finger grille.

They say that each firefly has its own flash sequence like a lighthouse. I let it go before noting its pattern and followed its staggering trail for a spell, while the dent of my palm still felt the illusory heat.

私がまた歩き始めた時

なんて思いがけないことだったろう
私がまた歩き始めたとき

風が海からではなく海の方へ
私の背中をそっと押した

足の下の砂が退いていく波と一緒に浚われて
私の膝が崩れた

波打ち際で私は溶けた
波にならされる砂の城のように

そこには初めから何もなかったのかもしれない
最後の微かなこぶが消えた

私がまた歩き始めたとき
私はずいぶん遠くへ行った

When I Started Walking Again

How unlooked for
when I started walking again.

Wind, not from, but towards the sea
pressed gently upon my back

and when the sand under my feet dredged away
with the retreating water, my knees collapsed.

I dissolved into the sand on the shore
like a sand-castle smoothened by waves.

The last small knob disappeared as if nothing
was ever there.

When I started walking again
I went pretty far.

イゾルト

イゾルトは墓石ではなく一本の木を望んだ
その願いは叶えられ
若い白樺が植えられた

墓地の境界の錆びた鉄塀のそば
繻子の光沢で白樺の葉っぱは震えた

「世界を満たす光」を返すために
そして空に一本の孤立した暗い染みを付けた

彼女は横たわり
ギータンジャリが胸の上で緩やかな切妻で開かれ
そのページに親指が挟まれている

ベンガル語で読みあげる彼女のお守りタゴールの『ギータンジャリ』
でも一体誰に

アロー　アマー、アロー　アゴー、　アロー　ブーゴン　ブーラ……

彼女は墓石ではなく一本の木を望んだ
その願いを叶えるために植えられた白樺
今はもう無い

墓の傍にはかつて巡礼の標となった円塔が聳え
今では遠い異国からの旅人たちが
こぞってその円錐の石屋根を見にやって来る

Iseult

Iseult asked for a tree not a gravestone
and her wish was honoured.
A young silver birch planted at her feet.

Those satiny leaves fluttered against
the rusty iron grille of the cemetery boundary,

to return the light, the world-filling light,
and stain dark the tree's lone shape, against the sky.

She rests herself and her book,
holding a gentle gable on her breast,
thumbs inserted in the opened page.

It's Tagore's Gitanjali, her talisman
and she recites in Bengali, but to who?

Alo amar, alo ogo, alo bhugon bhura ...

She asked for a tree not a headstone
and her wish was honoured with a birch,
but the tree is no more.

Nearby, the imposing medieval round tower,
once a pilgrim mark. Today, endless foreigners visit
to look up at its conical stone roof.

みてごらん
墓地の境界の赤く錆びた鉄塀近く
真新しい花崗岩の墓石に名が刻まれている
「イゾルト」と

円塔の影が濃くなっていく夕方
墓石に穿たれた小さな洞に鳩が一羽鳴いている
もの思わし気に右に首を傾けて

アロー　アマー、アロー　アゴー、　アロー　ブーゴン　ブーラ……
（光よ　私の光よ　世界を満たす光よ……）

注 ＊『ギータンジャリ』：「歌の捧げ物」を意味する。ベンガルの詩人、タゴール（1861−1941）の詩集。

Lo!
A granite headstone stands pristine at the boundary edge
of the rusty iron grille and her name inscribed
'Iseult'.

Under the deepening shadow of the tower
a pensive dove carved in the hollow of the stone,
lists to the right and cries

Alo amar, alo ogo, alo bhugon bhura ...
(Light, my light, the world-filling light ...)

Note: Gitanjali-song offerings: Poetry book by Bengalese Poet, Rabindranath Tagore (1861-1941).

一番遠くへ

　青い空、ツグミはそう思った。そうではなかった。
　それは即座に死んで私の手に感じられた温もりの失
われていくのもなんと素早かったことだろう。濡れた
小石のようなその眼を私は閉じてやった。それらには
窓ガラスの青が「空」と映ったのだ。だがそうではな
かった。空の向こう側からツグミを招んだのは何だっ
たのだろう。
　ある詩人がこう言った。

　野生動物が自分を哀れに思うのを見たことがない

　ああ、これがその野生の生き物。私はこの鳥の生を
知らず、その死だけを目撃したのだ。仲間はもうとっ
くに行ってしまった。海の向こうへ、山へ、砂漠へ、
森へ。この軽いつばさでどこへだって行ける筈だった。
仲間は彼を残して行ってしまった。
　いや、このツグミも行ったのだ。私の手の中にあっ
て、仲間よりも何マイルももっと遠い所へ、一番遠い
所へ。

To the Farthest

Blue sky, or so it thought, but not.

A thrush died outright and my hands still felt its last warmth, though fading fast. What was it there beyond the blue sky that called the thrush, I wonder? Now I close the pebble eyes that must have reflected that blue sky, or so it thought, but not.

A poet said:

I never saw a wild thing sorry for itself

This is that wild thing. I caught his death while knowing nothing about his life. The fellow birds have long gone. Their resilient, weightless wings can carry them anywhere, over sea, mountain, desert or forest. All other thrushes gone.

Yes, he has now gone too, in my hands, yet also somewhere, miles beyond his companions. Gone afar, to the farthest.

ブラドレー神父

長い廊下を一緒にダルガンハウスの食堂へ
ゆっくり歩いて行きながらブラドレー神父が訊いた
「コリドアッテ、ニホンゴデナンデシタカ」
「廊下です」と私は答えた、
「アア、ソーデシタ、ソーデシタ　ニホンゴ、ミナワスレマシタ
ナントハヤク　ヌケテイクコトデショウ」

長い廊下を歩きながら彼は考えていたに違いない
目にするすべての日本語を
階段、窓、壁、床、そして廊下……

誰もいない広い食堂で私たちは二人っきりで早い昼食をとった
「コンソメガイイデスカ　ポタージュガイイデスカ」
「コンソメがいいです」
「ボクモデス　コンソメノホーガズットイイデス」
神父は私の選択に満足したようだった

私たちは向かい合って座ってスープを啜った
「Londonッテイッテゴラン」
私の舌がRondonと言わないように意識してもつれた
「L…L…London!」
「ワルクナイヨ」と彼が言った
私がなんとかLondonと発音したので満足したようだった

Fr. Bradley

Walking slowly along the long corridor,
on the way to the dining room in Dalgan House,
Fr. Bradley asked 'What is corridor in Japanese?'
'Roka' said I.
'Oh, yes. Oh, yes. I have forgotten almost all my Japanese.
It is amazing how quickly it slips away.'

Walking along the corridor, he must have been thinking
of the Japanese word for everything he saw.
stairs, windows, walls, floor, ceiling, and corridor ...

We lunched alone in an enormous empty dining room.
He asked me if I want consommé or potage.
'Consommé' said I.
'So do I, consommé is much better.'
He seemed pleased with my choice.

We sipped it, sitting across the table from each other.
He asked me if I could say 'London'.
My tongue staggered in my mouth not to say 'Rondon'.
'L .. L .. London'
'Not bad', he said.
He seemed content I had managed to pronounce the 'L', almost.

次に彼に会った時、もう質問がなかった
ベッドに寝たきりで何も話さなかった
落ちくぼんだ目は大きく見開いて天井を見ているきりだった
ベッドの端に腰かけながら　私は思い出していた

彼がオシーンのように遂にアイルランドに戻って来たとき
若い頃に知っていた人たちは皆死んでしまったと言ったことを

「神父様、さようなら」日本語でそう耳元へささやくと
彼は二度三度、素早い瞬きをした
それが私のさよならへの思いがけない神父の返答だった

注＊ダルガンハウス：聖コロンバン会宣教師のセンター。
1941年に神学校として発足、現在は同会の本部並びに退職宣教師のホームと
先任宣教師の墓地を備える。

オシーン：ケルト民族の英雄。
「ティルナノグ」(常世の国)と呼ばれる国から故郷に戻ると
300年も経っていたという浦島太郎に似た話。

Next time when I visited, he neither asked me questions
nor spoke at all from his sick-bed.
His deep-set eyes wide open, looking fixedly at the ceiling.
Sitting beside his bed, I remembered that he once said that

all the people he knew as a young man, were long dead,
when he, like Oisín finally came back to Ireland.

When I whispered 'Sayonara, Fr. Bradley' in his ear, before
leaving, the eyes swiftly blinked a few times.
That was his unexpected response to my good-bye in Japanese.

Note: Dalgan House: Columban Missionary Fathers Centre.
Opened as a Seminary in 1941. Now an administration centre and
a retirement home and cemetery for missionaries.

Oisín: The Celtic hero returns to Ireland from Tír-na-nÓg, the Land of Eternal Youth.

初氷

指で突いて割った今年の冬の最初の氷
庭の水鉢に薄く張っている

子供の赤い霜焼けの手のような
カエデの葉っぱをつまんで引き上げた

これは最後に落ちた葉っぱの一枚だ
カエデは今は裸になって身を切る風の中に立っている

もう鳥たちを隠さない
雪の降りそうな空に十字を描いて

First Ice

I poked through the thin layer
of first ice on the bird-bath in the garden,

and picked out a maple leaf,
a child's red frostbitten hand

one of the last leaves that fell.
The tree now cleared full stands in a brisk wind.

It doesn't hide the birds anymore and
criss-crosses a sky that holds snow.

キツネの墓

　キツネが轢かれて路上に横たわっていた。通る車は次々とキツネを避けているようだった。血は見えなかった。

　夜の間、目が覚めるとキツネのことを考えていたので、翌朝、そこへ戻って行ってみた。キツネは消えてしまっていた。辺りを見渡した。車道で死んだ動物が何度も繰り返し轢かれることがないように誰かが路肩のほうに移動させたに違いなかった。そう思っている時、近くの草の広場に小さな盛り上がりを見つけた。キツネはそこに運ばれて埋められたのだ。盛り上がった部分は剥ぎ取った緑の芝のシートできちんと覆われている。

　それからまもなく、その盛り上がった部分はキツネが土の中に溶けてしまったかのように平らになった。それが草の広場のどこら辺りにあったのかさえ見分けがつかなくなった。なんて早く。

Fox's Grave

 A fox lay dead on the road. I saw the cars avoiding it. There was no blood.

 I went back there the following morning as I thought about the fox during the night each time I woke. It was gone. Somebody may have moved it to the shoulder not to be run over repeatedly, so I looked around. Then I noticed a small hump in the field nearby. So that's where he was. It was covered neatly with a sod of grass.

 In the following days, the raised part had flattened as if the fox had melted into the soil and the grave was not recognizable any more. So soon!

春に跪いて

膝が濡れたのは跪いたからだ
黄色いクロッカスと小さい水仙の写真を撮ろうと

ああ、それから青のクロッカスも
青は私の胸を締め付ける
去年もそうだった
それからその前の年もその前も……
お前の青が年ごとにもっと好きになる

この脆い青は嵐を切り抜けた
私の片膝を濡らしたのは
激しく降った雨にどっぷり飽和した春の地面だ

クリーム色のサクラソウ！
お前もみぞれや雪や強い雨を生き抜いた
雹にかじられもして
そう、この色こそが野に咲くサクラソウ
白でも、紫でも、紅でもない
静かなクリーム

私は跪いて
お前の顔に張り付いた去年の落ち葉を取り除ける
気づかれようとはしないで咲くおまえを
そのままそこにそっとしておこう

Genuflecting to Spring

Knee got wet as I knelt to take photos of
yellow crocus and dwarf narcissi.

Oh! Then blue crocus.
How your blue tightens my heart
as it did last year,
the year before that and ...
I love your blue more each year.

Blue flowers, look delicate yet survived storm Ciara
and the spring ground still saturated with heavy rain
made one knee wet.

Then cream primrose!
You, too survived sleet, snow and heavy showers
though gnawed by hail stones.
Yes, this is the colour for wild primrose,
not the white, nor the purple nor magenta.
This quiet colour, cream.

I kneel down to remove the dead leaves
of last year from your face.
You're not trying to be noticed.
I'll leave you where you are.

名前

　台所の戸棚の戸の裏側に一枚の紙きれが張り付けられている。セージ、ディル、ラヴィッジ……色々な名前が書きこまれている。憶えにくい名前というものがあって紙きれはカンニングペーパーみたいに助けになる。セントポーリア、ストレプトカーパス、ホーチュイニア　カメレオン……。名前はウイルスみたいに何処にでもありすべてに蔓延って、もし思い出せないと落ち着かない。

　何時だったか、私は本当の名前を思い出せなかった自分の白いバラに自分勝手に「雪の薄片」と名付けた。友だちがやって来てそのバラは「スーザン　ウイリアム　エリス」だと言った。その時、私はそれを否定した。自分で決めた嘘の名が頭に根を下ろしていたのだ。

　その夜の深夜に、彼女が正しいことを思い出した。そうだった、私は「スーザン　ウイリアム　エリス」を思い出した。その名前を！

Names

Stuck on the back of a kitchen press door, a piece of paper. Names of various things are written there. Sage, Dill, Lovage...certain names don't stick in my head and this helps me like a cheating paper. Saintpaulia, Streptocarpus, Houttuynia chameleon...names are everywhere like viruses, infesting everything and if I can't remember, I feel ill-at-ease.

Some time ago, I named a white rose of mine 'snow flakes', as a spur of the moment choice, not knowing the proper name. When a visiting friend called it 'Susan Williams-Ellis', alas! I denied her this, as my own invented name 'snow flakes' had long rooted in my head.

But that night at midnight, I realised she was right. Yes, I remembered 'Susan Williams-Ellis'. That name!

イェイツ姉妹

‘I’ と ‘A’ が ELIZABETH から、‘E’ と ‘S’ が YEATS から
墓石に嵌め込まれたメタルの文字が落ちてしまっている

失われた文字の跡を指でなぞってみる
象嵌はとても浅い

1940年に埋葬されたエリザベスは
一生の間ずっとロリーと呼ばれていた

妹の後に1949年に埋葬されたスーザンは
一生の間リリーと呼ばれていた

墓の傍に「7番目」と書かれた標識が立っている
郷土史家がこの地域のツアーをして7番目に立ち寄るのだ

彼はこんな風にいうだろうか……
「出版社を立ち上げたロリーと、刺繍家だったリリーは

仲が良くなかったが二人ともイェイツ一家を支えるために
生きている頃には懸命に働いた

『ダンドラムの風変わりな姉妹』
とバック・マリガンが言っている」

Two Spinsters

The 'I' and 'A' of ELIZABETH and 'E' and 'S' of YEATS,
inlaid metal letters, have fallen from the gravestone.

I place my finger in the gaps of those lost letters.
How shallow they were laid.

Elizabeth Corbet, known as Lolly all her life
was buried here in 1940.

Susan Mary, known as Lily all her life
followed her sister in 1949.

A small sign beside the grave says 'Stop No.7'. A local historian
gives a tour and stops here.

I wonder does he say that...
'Lolly a publisher and Lily an embroiderer didn't get on well.

That these sisters worked too hard to support
the Yeats' family, in their time.'

'The weird sisters of Dundrum'
as Buck Mulligan said.

墓地のある教会の裏の斜面はでこぼこしていて
二人の墓に誰かがすべすべした丸石をいくつか供えている

夏草が茂る頃には墓石が
長い草で埋まってしまうことがある

それでもダンドラムの高架で路面電車を待っている時
プラットフォームから彼女らの

墓がどこら辺りにあるか私にはわかっていて
独身だった姉妹のことを

生涯を通して懸命に働き続けた二人の姉妹のことを考える
'E' と 'S' の文字はどちらも落ちてしまっている

注＊スーザン（リリー）とエリザベス（ロリー）：アイルランド詩人イェイツ（1865−1939）の姉妹。

バック・マリガン：ジェイムズ・ジョイスの作品『ユリシーズ』に出て来る登場人物。
その中でイェイツ姉妹を「風変わりな姉妹」と形容した。

I see someone has been placing smooth round stones
on their grave, on the uneven slope, behind the church.

In Summer, sometimes the grass is so high
that it buries the headstones.

Even then, while waiting for a tram
at Dundrum bridge

from my elevated platform, I can spot their grave
in the distance and think of two spinsters,

who worked very hard all their lives, in those times.
'E' and 'S' of YEATS, both missing.

Notes: Susan (Lily) and Elizabeth (Lolly) : Sisters of the famous Irish Poet W.B. Yeats, (1865-1939).

Buck Mulligan: One of the characters in James Joyce's
'Ulysses', referred to the Yeats sisters as '..the weird sisters..'.

アパッチ

　同じ通りに住むフランクは「僕はアパッチだ」と言った。

　アリゾナ州から来たという彼のアメリカ風の郵便箱には「先住民」と書いてある。それには頭に羽の飾りをつけたアパッチの横顔が描かれている。彼は今のところ私が知っている唯一のアパッチだ。

　彼の飼っている犬は私が通り過ぎる度にひどく吠える。ある日、彼の犬があまりに吠えるのでこの大きな人が一体どうしたのかと、家から出てきたのだ。それが彼との最初の出会いだった。私は彼に犬の名を訊ねた。

「このチビはタイソンで僕はフランクだ」フランクはそう言って自分はアパッチだと付け加えた。握手をすると彼の大きな手が私の日本人の手を飲み込んだ。彼のお母さんはアパッチだったし、お父さんもアパッチで、祖父母もみなアパッチだったということだ。フランクの妻はアイリッシュ。一番小さくて声の大きい犬のタイソンは出自不明の雑種で、今でも私が通り過ぎる度にひどく吠えるのだ。

Apache

Frank, my neighbour said he was an Apache.

He came here from Arizona and his American post box says 'Native'. It shows the profile of an Apache in full head-dress. He is the only Apache I know, so far.

His small dog barked like mad each time I passed. One day this big man came out to see why. That was how we met first time. I asked him the name of the dog.

'This little one is Tyson and I am Frank.' Frank introduced himself as an Apache. My Japanese hand was swallowed by his, in our handshake. His mother was an Apache, his father was an Apache and his grandparents were all Apache. Frank's wife is Irish and Tyson, his dog of unknown type, smallest and loudest, still barks like mad when I pass there.

一対の靴

　一対の靴、一方の黒い方は汚れ、もう一方の明るい茶色は清潔に光っている。間違って履いた一対のように。それぞれの靴の主は、路面電車の通路側に座って足を組んだ。通路はとても狭く、二人の靴はペアのように並んだ。彼のは、たった今、殻から飛び出したばかりの栗の実のように光っている。

　私は釣り合わないそれらの靴をしばらく眺め通路越しに囁いた。

「あなたの靴はとてもきれいです。私は自分の靴が恥ずかしいです」

　彼はほほ笑んで言った。「僕はたった今朝、磨いたんですよ」。

　彼の目も光っていた。

A Pair of Shoes

A pair of shoes, one black and dirty, the other light-brown and polished. They look like an odd pair. The owners of each shoe sitting across the aisle from each other, both with knees crossed. The gap so narrow, our shoes aligned. His looked like a chestnut fresh out of the shell.

I stared at both for a short while and whispered to the stranger.

'Your shoes are so clean. I'm ashamed of mine'.

He smiled and said, 'I just did them this morning'.

His eyes sparkled, too.

さくら

　花をいっぱいにつけた桜の枝が路上に放りだされていた。誰かがいたずらに折って捨てたのだろう。ピンクの花はまだ新鮮だ。喜んで持ち帰ることにした。家へ帰る途中、角を曲がると同じ通りに住むマイケルが彼の犬と一緒にやって来るのと行き会った。立ち話をしていると、彼の犬が桜の花を食べ始めた。まあ！私はびっくりして枝を持ち上げた。でもそんなにひどいことではないのかもしれない。犬はこんなにきれいなものを食べたのだから。これも桜のもう一つの愛で方。私は花の少なくなった枝を持ち帰った。

Cherry Blossoms

 I found on the pavement a cherry tree sprig full of
blossoms. Someone must have snapped it off for a lark.
The pink flowers still fresh. Delighted to bring it
home with me. When I turned the corner, I met
Michael and his dog. While we chatted, the dog, ate
some of my cherry blossoms. Oops! I lifted the sprig
up higher. But it wasn't so bad, to see a dog eat such
pretty things. That's another form of admiration. I
just brought home a less flowered sprig.

ブディ
（ダブリン動物園生まれのベイビィエレファント、ブディに）

四本の脚
ブディにとっては多すぎる
右の前足は好奇心
でも左は臆病
後ろの右は頑固で
左は眠い
四本の脚はぶつかったりもつれたり

お前の耳はダンボみたいに
空を飛ぶには柔らかすぎる
お前の長い鼻は
母さんの足を一回りするには短すぎる
だけどひたいのまばらな毛は
お前を老いてとても賢く見せている

注＊ブディはインドネシア語で「賢い」の意。

Budi

(For Budi, the baby elephant, born in Dublin Zoo)

Four legs,
that's too many for Budi.
Front right is curious
but front left is reluctant.
Back right is stubborn
and back left is sleepy.
All collide and tangle.

Your ears are still too limp
to make you fly like Dumbo.
Your long nose is too short
to go all the way around Mommy's leg.
But the sparse hairs on your forehead
make you look old and very wise.

Note: In Indonesian language Budi means wise.

異星人

　この人を私はバスの窓からよく見かけたものだった。彼はいつもダンドラム交差点の角にあるキャンベル靴修理店の傍に立っていた。どんな季節でもどんな天候でも灰色のダッフルコートを着ていて片手で赤い花柄のマグカップを握り、もう一方の手をコートのポケットに入れていた。数えきれないほど何度も彼を見かけた。いつもバスの窓からだった。

　ある日、彼が私の乗っているバスに乗り込んできた。運転手に何か呟きバス代を払わなかった。彼は私と差し向かいになる席をとったので、私は初めて彼を真正面に間近に見ることになった。

　私はそれまで何度もバスの窓越しに見てきたこの人から目が離せなかった。夜であったので彼の方を見る度に窓ガラスに映った自分の顔も見ることになった。二つの顔、一つは実際の顔でもう一方は幻影だった。

　予期しないことにこの人は腕を私の方に延ばした。あまりに突然だったので私は一瞬怯えた。物乞いをするのだと思った。私は間違っていた。彼は深く窪んだ眼で自分の手をしみじみ眺め始めただけだった。初めに手の甲をそして手のひらを何度か返しながら。彼はそのことにすっかり心を奪われていた。彼は私の心を魅了する異星人だった。この異星人は彼の真正面にいる私の方をただの一度も見なかった。

　私たちはとても近かった。窓ガラスに映っているぼんやりとした私の顔は、バスの揺れによって、しばしば彼の現実の顔と重なった。その映像がじっと見つめ返してきたとき、私自身もまた異星人なのだと気がついたのだった。

Aliens

I used to see this man from the bus window. He was always standing at the corner of the Dundrum junction beside Campbell's shoe repair shop. He wore a grey duffle coat whatever the weather, or season. He was always holding out a ceramic mug with a red flower design in one hand and the other hand was always in the coat pocket. I saw him countless times, always through the bus window.

One day he boarded the bus which I was on. He mumbled something to the driver and didn't pay any bus fare. He sat exactly opposite from my own seat, so I saw him face to face for the first time, very close-up.

I couldn't stop watching this man I had seen so many times before, albeit through the bus window. As this was night time, when I looked his way, I could also see my own reflection in the glass window behind him. Two faces, one real and the other a simulacrum.

Unexpectedly, he stretched his hand in my direction. This was so sudden, that I was terrified for a second. Then I thought that he may be going to beg, but no, I was wrong. From his deep sunken eyes, he started examining his own hand. The back of it first, so keenly, then the palm, turning it over a few times. He was completely absorbed in this. A fascinating alien for me. The alien never once looked at me, although I was directly in front of him.

We were so close. My own ghostly reflection in the glass frequently overlapped with his real face, as the bus jostled along. As the image stared back at me, I realised that I too, was an 'alien'.

洗濯物

晴れた日に
洗濯物を干していると
自分自身も洗われて
きれいになって
日に干されているのだという
気分になる

泡の中で揉まれ
何度かすすがれ
きっちり絞られ
しわはしっかり伸ばされて
日に干されているのだという
気分に

ハエや蝶が
ひととき日向ぼっこする
うらおもてで
真っ裸

洗濯ばさみに
ちょっとつねられて

Hanging Washing

On a fine day
when I hang clothes,
I feel that I too, am drying myself
under the sun
after being washed
utterly clean.

Tossed about by the soapy water,
rinsed well
wrung out
creases stretched
then on the line
under the sun.

Flies and butterflies come to bask
for a moment.
I'm inside out
stark naked.

Pinched a little
by the pegs.

あとがき

　この詩集はたくさんの人の応援で出版されたものです。第五十五回小熊賞の知らせが届いたとき、家にいた息子が私を胴上げしました。彼はそのあと三日間ほど腰を痛めていました。今回、私はロックコンサートのシンガーが最後に聴衆の中に飛び込んでたくさんの手に支えられるように、数えきれない手で支えられました。小熊賞の先にまだ何かあるとは想像もしませんでした。生きている限り、思わぬことが起こるものです。人には新しい局面というものがいつもどこかにひっそり用意されているようです。この詩集はそのような一つの例として現れました。

　詩は十代から読んだり書いたりしていました。随分時が経ったものです。高校の文芸部の先輩が卒業していくときに一冊の詩集を下さいました。それは一九六三年に人文書院から発行された『ボードレール全集』の第一巻で福永武彦が訳したものです。その中の「陽気な死人」はこのように始まっています。

104 　　　蝸牛の這いまわるねばねばした地面に、

　　　　僕は自ら深い深い穴を掘ろう、

　　　　そこにのんびり古ぼけた骨を埋めて、

　　　　忘却の中に眠ろう、鱶が波間に眠るように。

　これは究極の平穏を希求した詩です。何故か私は圧倒されてしばらく「蝸牛」や「古ぼけた骨」や「眠る鱶」のことばかり考えたものです。この『雨の合間』の最初に「カタツムリ」という詩を選んだのは、十代の私がこの詩から受けた衝撃を記念するためでした。

　ダブリンに住み始めた頃、英語に訳されたボードレールの詩集を買い、「陽気な死人」を探して読みました。福永訳を読んだような衝撃は受けませんでした。それは、私の英語力の無さや英訳のせいばかりではなく、日本語の訳者、福永にはボードレールの憑依を可能にする性質があったからでしょう。「翻訳の仕上げは妖精がする」と、どこかで読みました。言い換えると、もし訳者がその可能性に対して開かれているならば、この世ならぬものからの霊感を得るということです。私も妖精の不思議な力を得るためにもう少し生きてみなければなりません。

随分早くから詩を書いて来たにも拘らず、私は自分が書いた詩を日本の詩雑誌へ投稿するという発想はありませんでした。ところが、アイルランドに来て十年ほど経った頃、英語で詩を書き始め、詩人のダーモット・ボルジャー氏がポエトリーワークショップをするという新聞記事を見つけた時、それに参加したいと思ったのでした。応募者は十篇の詩を送り、ボルジャー氏がそれを基に受講者を選ぶということでした。運良く、その受講者に選ばれ、彼の教室に数週間、通いました。素晴らしい経験でした。そこにあったのは激励だけでした。受講者の詩を一つ一つ丁寧に読んで、良い点を指摘、解説していきました。彼は有名な詩人の詩の例を一つも持ち出すことなく、むしろ私たちを詩人として扱いました。このあと、ボルジャー氏自らが私の二篇の詩、「台風」と「風の花嫁」をヘネシー賞に送り、それらが最終候補になりました。この初期の二篇は、以後、私が書いたすべての詩につながっているように思います。

　それから十年以上経って、二〇一四年に私の最初の二ヵ国言語詩集『アイルランドの風の花嫁』が出版されました。私が英語で書いた詩を、主に大学でアイルランド文学を教える諸先生が日本語に翻訳したものでした。これは、当時、日本ジェイムズ・ジョイス協会の会長であった、結城英雄氏の働きかけによるものでした。この二冊目の『雨の合間』によって、私の詩作が続いていることをかつての翻訳者の諸先生に示すことができるのは大きな安堵です。九年かかったのですけれど。また、ボルジャー氏にこの詩集へのコメントを頂けたのも喜びです。

　夫が「この詩集は『死』ばかり扱っている」と言ったので数えて見ると、四十のうち十七篇がそうでした。確かにボードレールの「陽気な死人」から受けた十代の衝撃と感銘が連綿と私の中で生き続けたとは言えるでしょう。「死」を扱うのは「生」を扱うことです。この二つは背中合わせであることを、日本人はみな知っています。「生きていく」根源的な力を人は何処から得るのでしょう。それが関心の一つとしてありました。それにしても、日本語では「詩」と「死」が、「想像」と「創造」が同じ音を持っているのは偶然ではないと思うのです。読者の皆さん、ユーモアのある作品も見つけてください。あります。

この詩集では日本語も英語も自分でやりました。英語から始まったものが多いのですが、日本語からの詩、また同時進行で書かれたものもあります。翻訳の都合上、二つの言語は影響し合い、英語の方を変えたり、日本語の方を変えたり、政治のような妥協がありました。異なる二つの言語を共存させるということは、異なる二人の人間が共存していく難しさと同じであり、時には行き詰まりも感じました。でも、それ以上に大きな発見と学びと驚きがあったのです。発見と学びと驚きなしでは、私は生きていけないことでしょう。

　この新版のクラウドファンディングプロジェクトを支援してくださったすべての皆様、ありがとうございます。ダーモット・ボルジャー、逢坂巌、栩木伸明、早川健治、柴田望、結城史郎、河野さとみ、諸氏のこれまでの激励に深く感謝致します。この詩集の擁護者として初めから前線に立って下さったアーサー・ビナードさんに、心からお礼申し上げます。装丁に鈴木成一さん、装画に朝光ワカコさんを得たことは願ってもない私の幸運でした。とりわけ、この出版企画のプロジェクターとして、全行程を情熱と忍耐で歩き通して下さったミツイパブリッシングの中野葉子さん、感謝の気持ちでいっぱいです。この出版は貴方が実現させました。

ダブリンにて

津川エリコ

106

Afterword

This collection of poems was published with the support of many people. When I received the news of the 55th Oguma Award, my son, who was at home, lifted me up in his arms. He had a backache for three days after that. This time, I was supported by countless hands, just as a singer at a rock concert is supported by many hands when he jumps into the audience at the end. After receiving the Oguma Award, I didn't imagine that there would be something further to come. Unexpected things happen throughout our lives. It seems that there is always a new phase of our lives waiting for us somewhere. This project is an example of that.

I have been reading and writing poetry since I was a teenager. A long time has passed since then. I remember that a senior pupil from my high school literature club presented me with a book of poems when he graduated. It was the first volume of Baudelaire's complete works, published by Jinbun-shoin in 1963 and translated by Takehiko Fukunaga. In that book, 'The Grateful Dead' begins like this;

On the sticky ground where the snails crawl,
I will dig myself a deep, deep hole,
And bury my old bones there, at leisure,
And sleep in oblivion, like a shark sleeps among the waves.

This poem expresses a wish for ultimate peace. For some reason, I was overwhelmed with thoughts of 'snails', 'old bones,' and 'sleeping sharks'. I chose my poem 'Snail' as the opening poem in my book 'Lull in the Rain' to commemorate the impact that poem had on me as a teenager. A long time has passed.

When I started living in Dublin, I bought a book of Baudelaire's poems translated into English and sought out 'The Grateful Dead' to read. It didn't have the same impact on me as the first time, when I read Fukunaga's Japanese translation. This was not because of my own poor English ability or the English translation itself, but because the Japanese translator, Fukunaga, had allowed Baudelaire to inhabit him. I read somewhere that 'translation is finished by the fairies.' In other words, if a translator is open to it, he or she can get some otherworldly inspiration. I myself must live a little longer to gain the wondrous power of the fairies.

Even though I had been writing poetry for a long time, I had never thought of submitting my poems to Japanese poetry magazines. However, about ten years after arriving in Ireland, I began writing poetry in English. At one point, I came across a newspaper article about a poetry work-shop being offered by the poet Dermot Bolger. This interested me. Applicants were to send in ten poems, and Mr. Bolger would choose the participants based on the work. As luck would have it, I was chosen and attended his class for several weeks. It was a wonderful experience. There was only encouragement there. Mr Bolger, carefully read each of our poems, pointing out and explaining the good points. He didn't refer to any famous poets, but treated us as poets.

After the work-shop, Mr. Bolger submitted two of my poems, *Typhoon* and *Bride of the Wind*, to the Hennessy Literary Awards, where they were short-listed. I feel that those two early poems, hold the essence of whatever I have written since.

More than ten years later, in 2014, my first bilingual collection of poetry was published. Those poems which I wrote in English were translated into Japanese by various professors, most of whom teach Irish literature at Japanese universities. Mr. Hideo Yuki, who was president of the James Joyce society of Japan, at the time, arranged it all. It was a great relief for me, to be able to show to those translators, by publishing my second collection of poems, 'Lull in the Rain', that I was continuing my writing. Even if it took me nine more years to do so. Also, I must say that I am very glad, that Mr. Bolger has kindly given comment for this second collection.

On reading 'Lull in the Rain' my husband said to me, 'This collection is all about death,' and sure enough, when I checked, that was true for seventeen out of the forty poems in it. So, the impact I received as a teenager, from Baudelaire's 'The Grateful Dead' has continued to live on in me. To deal with death is to deal with life. All Japanese know that the two go hand-in-hand. Where do people get the basic strength to 'live'? That is one of my interests. I don't think it is a coincidence that 'poetry' and 'death' have the same sound in Japanese, as do 'imagination' and 'creation'. Readers! Please find the humorous poems. They are there too!

In this latest collection of poems, I wrote both the Japanese and the English myself. Many of the poems started out in English, but there are also poems which began in Japanese and some written simultaneously in both. For the convenience of translation, the two languages influenced each other, and just as in politics, compromises were made in both languages. The co-existence of two different languages is like the difficulty of co-existence of two different peoples, and I sometimes felt an impasse. But more often, there were great discoveries, learning and surprises, without which, I would not be able to live my life.

I would like to thank each of you who supported this re-publishing project through the crowd-funding. Thanks sincerely to Dermot Bolger, Iwao Osaka, Nobuaki Tochigi, Kenji Hayakawa, Nozomu Shibata, Shiro Yuki and Satomi Kono for their encouragement. Special thanks to Arthur Binard who has been an advocate for this publication from the start. It was my great fortune to have Seiichi Suzuki who did the overall design and Wakako Asamitsu for her cover artwork. Particular thanks go to Yoko Nakano of Mitsui Publishing for her enthusiasm and patience throughout this publishing journey. She made this happen.

Eriko Tsugawa
In Dublin

津川エリコ

北海道釧路市生まれ。ダブリン在住。『雨の合間』で第55回小熊秀雄賞受賞。小説「オニ」で第56回北海道新聞文学賞受賞。著書に詩集『アイルランドの風の花嫁』（金星堂）、随筆集『病む木』（デザインエッグ）、アイルランドの詩集アンソロジー 'Landing Places' (Dedalus Press) などに作品所収。

Eriko Tsugawa

Born in Kushiro city and now a resident of Dublin. She won the 55th Oguma Award for her poetry collection, *Lull In The Rain*. Her novella *Oni* won the 56th Hokkaido Shimbun Literary award. She is the author of another poetry collection, *Bride of the Wind* (Kinseido), an essay collection *The Sick Tree* (Design Egg) and has been included in several Irish poetry anthologies, notably, *Landing Places* (Dedalus press) among others.

雨　の　合　間
Lull in the Rain

2024年3月25日　新版第1刷発行

著者
津川エリコ

ブックデザイン
鈴木成一デザイン室

装画
朝光ワカコ

発行者
中野葉子

発行所
ミツイパブリッシング
〒078-8237 北海道旭川市豊岡7条4丁目4-8
トヨオカ7・4ビル 3F-1
電話 050-3566-8445
E-mail: hope@mitsui-creative.com
http://www.mitsui-publishing.com

印刷・製本
モリモト印刷